For Robert

PUBLISHED IN 2016 by
LAURENCE KING PUBLISHING LTD.
361-373 CITY ROAD
LONDON EC1V 1LR
TEL: + 44 20 7841 6900
FAX: + 44 20 7841 6910
www.laurenceking.com
enquiries@laurenceking.com

A CATALOG RECORD OF THIS BOOK IS
AVAILABLE FROM THE BRITISH LIBRARY.

ISBN 978-1-78067-767-5

Printed in China.

Thanks to:

Alex Coco, Felicity Awdry,
Laurence, Jo and Elizabeth, LKP.
Louise Kuenzler, Sophie McKenzie (City Lit)
David Lucas
Elizabeth Sheinkman WME
Hamish and Alexander
ANGUS HYLAND.

Bob

The Artist

Written and Illustrated by
Marion Deuchars

LAURENCE KING

"What a beautiful day for a walk on my FINE legs," said Bob.

"Oooh!
Look at that
FUNNY
STICK WALK",
said OWL.

This teasing
made Bob
VERY SAD.

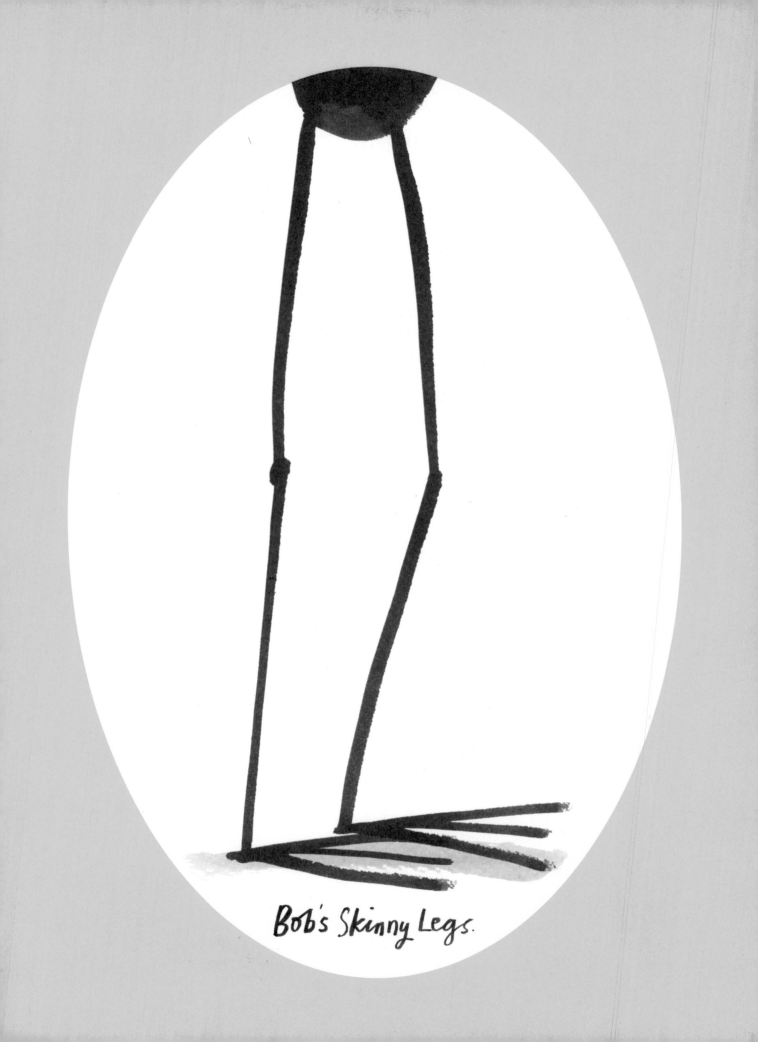

Bob's Skinny Legs.

But that did not work.

"I know. I'll EAT my legs bigger."

But he felt ridiculous.

Bob went for a long walk.

BOB had a BRILLIANT IDEA.
He got his PAINTS out and
started to COLOR his BEAK.

On Monday he painted like MATISSE in BEAUTIFUL colorful patterns.

"OOOh!
HoW EXQUISITE!
A GENIUS!
Incredible!
SuCH DARING!
AMAZING CoLoR!
STuPENDouS!
BRILLIANT!
A work of ART,"
said Owl.

On TUESDAY Bob painted his beak in BRIGHT SPLATTERS like the painter JACKSON POLLOCK.

"WOW! what an INCREDIBLE beak," said Cat.

And so NOW EVERY DAY Bob paints his beak in a different way.

Bob LOVES showing off his
WONDERFUL beak designs.
He doesn't worry about his
SKINNY legs any more.
IN FACT, he is now
rather PROUD of them!

AND sometimes, Bob EVEN likes to leave his beak RED.

"What an ELEGANT walk!" said Owl.

"GREAT legs!" said Cat.

"How minimal!"